NOT JUST ANOTHER MOOSE

Stephanie Greene • illustrated by Andrea Wallace

MARSHALL CAVENDISH
New York

Text copyright © 2000 by Stephanie Greene
Illustrations copyright © 2000 by Andrea Wallace
All rights reserved
Marshall Cavendish, 99 White Plains Road, Tarrytown, New York 10591

Library of Congress Cataloging-in-Publication Data
Greene, Stephanie.
Not just another moose / by Stephanie Greene ; illustrated by Andrea Wallace.
p. cm.
Summary: When Moose's magnificent antlers fall off, he discovers he has other
remarkable features as well.
ISBN 0-7614-5061-0
[1. Moose—Fiction.] I. Wallace, Andrea, ill. II. Title.
PZ7.G8434No   2000   99-41355   [E]—dc21   CIP

The text of this book is set in 14 point Cheltenham Light.
The illustrations are rendered in pen-and-ink and watercolor.

Printed in Hong Kong
First edition
6 5 4 3 2 1

To Marnie — S. G.

For John — A. W.

DISASTER STRIKES

Even for a moose, Moose was funny-looking.

His eyes were as tiny as marbles.

His nose looked like a huge baked potato.

His knees knocked.

But nobody noticed how funny-looking Moose was. And all because of his antlers.

They swept up toward the sky like huge hands cupped to catch the rain. They stretched five feet from tip to tip.

They made Moose feel very special.

To a moose, having big antlers is as important as having big muscles is to a man.

Everyone respects you.

Everyone wants to be your friend.

So, of course, the day they fell off was the worst day of Moose's life.

He was standing by the lake. He had just admired his reflection on the water.

Suddenly, Moose felt his antlers totter.

Then he felt them wobble.

Then he didn't feel them at all.

But he did hear a *thud*.

Moose looked down and saw his magnificent antlers lying on the ground.

He felt his head. It was bare.

He looked around for help. He was alone.

So Moose did the only thing he could think of. He ran home and called his mother.

As soon as he heard her voice, he felt better. When she laughed at his story, he felt worse.

"My darling Moose," she said, "that's what happens to a moose's antlers. They fall off every fall. And they grow back every spring. They'll be back next year, bigger than ever."

She asked him if he was taking his vitamins. She told him to wash behind his ears. By the time Moose hung up, he was sadder than ever.

It was clear his mother didn't understand.

Without his antlers, he was just another moose.

A FRIEND IN NEED

When the doorbell rang, Moose threw a towel over his head.

"Nobody's home," he yelled.

"Then who are you?" said a voice. It was Hildy, his best friend. "Come on, Moose, let me in."

Moose thought quickly. "I can't. I'm planning a surprise."

"What kind of surprise?" said Hildy.

"A surprise surprise," Moose said. "Come back in the spring."

"The spring! Come on, Moose, what's going on in there?" She banged on the door.

"Please," Moose pleaded. "I need my privacy. Don't go away mad, Hildy, just go away."

"Okay."

Moose heard footsteps. He put his ear to the door.

"I'm going," Hildy called. She sounded far away. "It's safe to come out now."

Moose waited a minute. Then he opened the door.

Hildy was standing on the front stoop.

"I tricked you," she said. She put her foot in the door so Moose couldn't close it.

"Come on, Moose, let me in."

Then she stopped. "What's that, a new hat?"

Moose took off the towel. "Go ahead, laugh."

"What have you done to yourself?" Hildy looked at him closely. "I know! You did something to your eyes."

She sounded pleased. "Why, you've got the prettiest little eyes I've ever seen, Moose."

Moose fluttered his eyelashes up and down.

"And your legs. I never noticed you had such muscular legs."

Moose looked down. His legs *did* look strong.

"It's my antlers," he said. "They fell off."

"Why so they did," Hildy said. "And good riddance to them. If you don't mind my saying, they were kind of big."

"Kind of big?" said Moose. "They were HUGE."

"That was the problem," said Hildy. "Remember the time you got stuck in my living room? And the time you broke my grandmother's lamp?"

Moose remembered, all right. He was standing in her front hall. He had turned his head to say something.

He could still hear the awful *crash*!

"Well, okay," Moose said. "But don't get too used to it. They're going to grow back in the spring."

"Fine," said Hildy. "Then tonight is the perfect night for you to come for dinner. I came to invite you, but I thought we'd have to eat outside."

When Moose got to Hildy's house, she handed him a box.
Inside was a fuzzy blue hat with ear flaps.

"It's to keep your new head warm," she said.

Moose tied the flaps under his chin. The hat was warm and soft. He
wore it while he ate. He wore it while they played checkers.

And even though Hildy won every game, Moose's little eyes
sparkled like diamonds the whole time.

"THERE'S NOTHING TO DO"

It was hunting season.

Moose hated hunting season.

For weeks on end, he had to stay indoors.

All he could do was read books. Or do puzzles. Or draw pictures.

After a while, it got very boring.

Hildy came to say good-bye. She gave him a new set of colored pencils.

"Gee, thanks," Moose said. He loved to draw. He was very good at it. Hildy wasn't nearly as good, but Moose always gave her encouragement.

"There's no good or bad in art," he told her. "There are just different styles."

It made Hildy feel better.

"Draw me a picture," she said when she left.

"I'll draw you a month of pictures," Moose said in a gloomy voice. "There's nothing else to do."

The first week, Moose read all his books. He made grilled cheese. He drew pictures.

And every day, he peered at the top of his head in the mirror.

Nothing was happening.

Finally, he ran out of things to do.

"I've got to think of something," he said.

He went into the kitchen to make some hot chocolate. He ate a donut, too. It made him feel a little better.

Eating one of his homemade donuts always did. They were delicious. Crisp on the outside, soft on the inside.

"I could sell these," Moose said to himself.

That's when his idea was born.

MOOSE MAKES MONEY

Early the next morning, a hunter was walking quietly through the woods.

It was cold and foggy. He had to move slowly. Three steps, then stop and listen. Three more steps, then stop and listen again.

The hunter was cold and hungry.

He was feeling sorry for himself, too.

He hadn't seen a single moose all season.

He bet they had all gone on vacation. They were probably lying on a beach, sipping fancy drinks and eating tortilla chips.

Suddenly, he sniffed the air. Coffee.

"I must be going crazy," he thought. "Maybe I'm freezing to death."

He forgot to walk quietly. He stumbled forward into a small clearing.

There was a table in front of him. A sign said HOT COFFEE AND HOMEMADE DONUTS, 25 CENTS.

Moose was behind it. He was wearing a white apron and his blue hat. The hunter rubbed his eyes.

"You sure look cold and hungry," said Moose. "How about some coffee?"

He poured a cup and gave it to the hunter. "You might like to try one of my homemade donuts, too. I'm famous for them."

"Say, aren't you a moose?" said the hunter.

Moose laughed. "Have you ever heard of a moose who cooks?"

"No, I guess not," the hunter said.

"Here, try a donut," Moose said.

The hunter bit into it. It was the best donut he had ever tasted.

"This is great," he said, "but I'd still swear you're a moose."

"When is a moose not a moose?" Moose said quickly. "When he's an artist."

He whipped around a large square of cardboard that was standing behind him. It said ORIGINAL ARTWORK 1 DOLLAR.

"Gee, this stuff is good," the hunter said with surprise. "You did all these?"

Moose nodded.

"I wish I could draw," the hunter said. "I'm terrible in art."

"There's no such thing as good or bad in art," Moose said. "There are just different styles."

"I never looked at it that way before," said the hunter. "That makes me feel better."

He bought three pictures and a bag of donuts.

"You'd better watch out for some of these other hunters," he said as he left. "Some people don't know good art when they see it."

The day hunting season ended, Moose knocked on Hildy's door.

"Moose!" She gave him a big hug. "Was it terrible? Were you lonely?"

"Why, no, I had a wonderful time," said Moose. "I sold my pictures to a hunter."

"Oh, sure." Hildy laughed. "I suppose you had coffee and donuts with him, too."

"As a matter of fact, I did," said Moose.

"I'm so glad hunting season is over," Hildy said. "I've missed your sense of humor."

STOLEN PROPERTY

It was the first day of spring.

Moose always went bird-watching on the first day of spring.

He hopped out of bed at five o'clock. He put his binoculars around his neck.

He put his bird book into a bag and grabbed a few donuts.

Then he walked into the woods.

Being a moose made bird-watching easy. Birds weren't afraid of him. They didn't fly away when they saw him.

In fact, back when he had antlers, they used to sit on his points and go for a ride.

This morning, he peered through his binoculars. He made notes in his bird book.

He sat on a moss-covered rock and ate a donut.

One minute everything was peaceful. The next minute, it wasn't.

There was a tremendous crash in the bushes.

Then a loud rustling.

It sounded as if something heavy was headed straight for him.

Before Moose could move, the hunter burst through the trees and into the clearing.

He was dragging a pair of antlers. They were five feet wide from tip to tip.

Moose jumped to his feet.

The hunter jumped, too.

He saw a huge moose standing in front of him. He thought about screaming. He thought about running.

Instead, he held on tighter to the antlers.

Moose and the hunter stood face to face, nose to nose.

Finally, Moose spoke.

"I believe those antlers are mine."

A NEW BACKPACK

"No, they're not. They're mine," the hunter said. He looked from the spots on Moose's forehead to the antlers on the ground. "They're mine," he said again. "I found them."

"Yes, but I lost them," said Moose.

"Finders keepers, losers weepers," said the hunter.

"What are you going to do with them?" asked Moose.

The hunter had to think quickly.

He didn't want to tell Moose he was going to hang them above his fireplace and pretend he'd shot a moose.

Instead, he said, "I'm going to use them to carry things."

"You are?" said Moose. "How?"

"Like this." The hunter took a rope from his backpack.

He took the antlers and heaved them onto his head.

He tied the rope under his chin. "See?"

"Very clever," said Moose. "What are you going to carry?"

The hunter took his pocketknife out of his pack and hung it on a point.

He took out a canteen and hung it from another point.

Then he hung a compass, a pack of matches, and his lunchbox from the other points.

"You're right," said Moose. "That looks very convenient."

"It's a little heavy," said the hunter.

"Oh, don't I know," said Moose. He looked at the hunter's pack. "I guess you don't need that anymore."

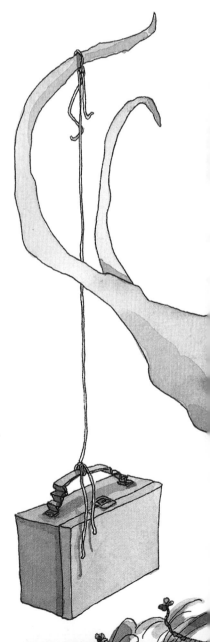

The hunter couldn't look down with the antlers on his head.

"I guess not," he said. "You might as well take it."

"Why, thank you," Moose said. "I sure can use it."

Moose put his bird book, his binoculars, and his donuts into the pack. He put it on his back.

"Gee, this is comfortable," he said. "Of course, it's not as convenient as your antlers."

"No, of course not," said the hunter. "Well, I'd better get going. Good-bye."

"Good-bye," Moose said. "You may get a few hitchhikers on those empty points of yours."

"Ha-ha," the hunter said. "That's a good one."

Then he staggered off into the woods.

THE RETURN OF THE ANTLERS

Moose was drinking from the lake when he saw them.

Two tiny stumps covered with a thin skin like velvet.

His antlers.

He leaped into the air and clicked his heels together.

Soon, he'd be special again.

Everyone would admire him.

He did a little dance.

"What are you so happy about?" said a glum voice.

Moose spun around.

The hunter was sitting on a stump. He didn't look happy.

"My antlers," Moose said, blushing. "They're growing back."

"Big deal," said the hunter. "I've got the biggest set you've ever seen, hanging on my wall."

"You do?" said Moose. He stepped closer. The hunter looked up at Moose towering above him.

"I bought them in a store," he said quickly. "I'm a fishérman." He held up his fishing rod.

"I can see that," said Moose. "How *is* the fishing?"

"Not so good." The hunter looked gloomy again. "I tied up my boat, but it got loose."

The hunter pointed. Moose saw a small boat out in the middle of the lake.

"I can get it for you," he said.

"You can?"

"Sure," Moose said. "Moose are very strong swimmers, you know."

Without another word, Moose dove into the water. He paddled out to the boat and climbed in.

"Now what?" he shouted.

"Row!" shouted the hunter.

"What's 'row'?"

The hunter made rowing motions with his arms.

"Oh-h-h-h." Moose picked up the oars and rowed. In no time, he was back at shore. The hunter grabbed the boat and pulled it in.

"Thanks a lot," he said. "I didn't know what to do. That water is freezing."

"I know," said Moose, "it feels great."

The hunter looked at Moose closely. "Haven't I seen you somewhere before?"

"You know what they say about moose," said Moose. "You've seen one, you've seen them all."

"Whoever said that didn't know moose," said the hunter. "Not the way I do."

"What do you mean?"

"Every moose I ever met was different."

"It was?"

"Sure. I met one last year who was a great artist."

"Really?"

"Yep. The one I met this spring was very funny. He told me an antler joke."

"No kidding."

"And now you," said the hunter. "You're a pretty good dancer."

"Why, thank you," said Moose.

"Take it from me," said the hunter. "There's no good or bad with moose, there are just different styles."

"Gee, I never looked at it that way before," said Moose. "That makes me feel better."

The hunter climbed into his boat. "By the way," he said casually, "how big do you think your antlers will be this year?"

"Pretty big," said Moose.

"You don't say." The hunter picked up the oars. "Maybe I'll see you around."

"Not if I see you first," said Moose.

The hunter laughed, "Ha-ha, that's a good one."